A FIRST THESAURUS

By Harriet Wittels
and
Joan Greisman

A GOLDEN BOOK • NEW YORK
Western Publishing Company, Inc.
Racine, Wisconsin 53404

For Brad, Sherry, Mark, Adam, Craig, and Amy

Introduction

Riddle: What sounds like Brontosaurus, but is found on a bookshelf near the dictionaries, not at the natural history museum?

Answer: A thesaurus, of course! A thesaurus is a book that lists synonyms—words that have almost the same meaning; and antonyms—words of opposite meaning. **A First Thesaurus** will give you many accurate, interesting, and colorful new words to use, in addition to the old ones you already know. You will find this book useful, helpful, practical, handy, valuable, and beneficial. That is its aim, purpose, goal, object, and target.

Using the Thesaurus

Entry Words

The words in **A First Thesaurus** that have synonyms and antonyms are called **entry words**. They are listed in alphabetical order, and printed in dark type:

> **bleak** dreary, dismal cheerful
> **blend** mix, combine, join separate
> **bless** praise, thank, glorify curse

Look in the "A" section. What entry word comes just before **accident**? (Answer: **accept**.) Now look in the "B's." What entry word comes right after **brand**? Look in the "C's." Between which two entry words do you find **car**?

Guide Words

The two words at the top of every page, in dark type, are called **guide words**. They are the first and last entry words on each page, and they will "guide" you to all the entry words between them.

Here's an example: If the guide words were **change** and **chop**, you would find the entry word **chest** on that page. But you would not find the entry word **climb** on that page. Now look up the entry word **decide**. What are the two guide words at the top of the page?

Synonyms

Synonyms are words that have the same, or almost the

same, meaning. Here are two groups of synonyms:

embarrassed ashamed, humiliated, mortified
embrace grasp, hug, hold, clutch

Synonyms can usually be substituted for one another in a sentence:

fad style, fashion, craze, rage
Blue jeans are now the fad.
Blue jeans are now the style.
Blue jeans are now the fashion.
Blue jeans are now the craze.
Blue jeans are now the rage.

But sometimes synonyms cannot be substituted for one another in a sentence. Look at this group:

match contest, game, battle
Today we had a spelling match in our class.
Today we had a spelling contest in our class.
Today we had a spelling game in our class.

But you wouldn't say:
Today we had a spelling battle in our class.

When you look up a word in this book, you may find that not all of the synonyms fit correctly in your sentence. You'll have to use common sense and good judgment in choosing the right word.

Antonyms

A word that has the opposite meaning to that of the entry

word is called an **antonym**. You will find it in red, at the end of a group of synonyms:

> **like** enjoy, admire, appreciate   dislike
> **misty** cloudy, foggy, smoky   clear

Here's an example:

> She doesn't like <u>short</u> hair, so she wears hers <u>long</u>.

The word "long" is the antonym of the word "short."

Now you try. Look up the entry word in dark type and find the antonyms to complete these sentences:

> Cinderella was **beautiful**, but her stepsisters were
> _____.
> It takes longer to **pack** the car than to _____ it.

Entry Words With More Than One Meaning

Some entry words, like **tag**, have more than one meaning. Tag could mean follow, shadow, trail, pursue, or tail. But tag could also mean label, name, or brand. That's why tag has two numbers for the two groups of synonyms. Here's another example:

> **tape** 1. wrap, bind, tie
> **tape** 2. record

In this book, the entry word **run** has five numbers for its five different meanings. Look up the entry word **run**, and in the following sentences, find the number of the correct group of synonyms.

The computer can only <u>run</u> on electricity. (Answer: 3.)
Will Tom <u>run</u> for class president this term? (?)
Susan had to <u>run</u> to catch the bus. (?)
Let the water <u>run</u> until it's cold. (?)
Our principal knows how to <u>run</u> our school. (?)

Entry Words That Are Spelled the Same

Some entry words are spelled the same, but we say them differently and they have completely different meanings. That's why these words have different numbers in front of them. Look at the two entry words below and how they are used.

1. **minute** instant, moment
2. **minute** tiny, small, miniature   giant
   Billy's dog runs to him the <u>minute</u> he whistles. (**1.**)
   You must use a microscope to see those <u>minute</u>
      germs. (**2.**)

Now see if you can complete the sentences below with the correct entry word and its number.

1. **close** shut, fasten, lock   open
2. **close** near, approaching   far
   School children love the month of June, because
      summer vacation is _____.
   Please _____ the door behind you.

That's how **A First Thesaurus** works. It's easy and fun. Use it often. Make it a habit and you'll find that it will help to improve your reading, your writing, and your speech.

A

abandon   desert, forsake, leave

ability   skill, talent, know-how   inability

abnormal   odd, unnatural, irregular   normal

about   1. almost, nearly, approximately, around

about   2. concerning, of

abrupt   sudden, unexpected   expected

absent   away, truant   present

absorb   take in, soak up, sponge

absurd   unbelievable, ridiculous, ludicrous   sensible

abuse   mistreat, damage

accept   adopt, believe, approve, consent to   deny

accident   mishap, fluke

accomplish   complete, do, carry out, finish, achieve

account   story, reason, description, statement

accumulate   collect, assemble, gather, compile,
  store up

accurate   correct, right, perfect   inaccurate, wrong

accuse   blame, charge

actor

ache pain, throb, hurt

achieve accomplish, fulfill

act perform, behave

active lively, peppy, spirited, energetic inactive, lazy

actor performer, entertainer

actual real, true, genuine, authentic

add put together, join subtract

adequate enough, sufficient, satisfactory insufficient

admire like, respect, appreciate

admit 1. confess, acknowledge deny

admit 2. allow to enter, receive

adore love, worship, idolize, cherish, revere hate

adult grown-up, mature immature, juvenile

advance proceed, progress, further recede

advertise announce, publicize, promote

advise suggest, recommend, direct, counsel

affair 1. happening, occasion, occurrence, event, party, festivity

affair 2. business, concern, interest

affection liking, fondness dislike

afraid frightened, scared, alarmed unafraid, fearless

again once more, another time

agony   suffering, pain, distress, torture

agree   consent to, comply with, approve of   disagree, differ with

agreement   pact, contract, treaty, bargain, deal, understanding

aid   help, assist, support, serve   hinder

aim   purpose, goal, object, target

alarm   scare, frighten, startle, shock, unnerve   calm, soothe

alert   wide-awake, watchful, ready   dull

alibi   excuse, story

allow   permit, let   forbid, deny

allowance   allotment, grant, budget

almost   about, nearly, approximately, practically

alone   solitary, isolated, sole

also   too, in addition, besides, as well

always   forever, for good, for keeps   never

amend   change, correct, improve

among   surrounded by, amid, in with

amount   sum, quantity

amusing   funny, entertaining, delightful, comical, humorous   boring, dull

anchor   1. fasten, fix, secure, attach

anchor   2. ship hook

anchor (2)

ancient old, aged, antique modern, new

angry furious, enraged, annoyed, cross

animal beast, creature

announce state, broadcast, proclaim, make known

annoy bother, disturb, tease, irritate, anger, pester, provoke

answer reply, response question

apparel clothing, dress, garments, attire

appear 1. seem, look

appear 2. arrive, approach, enter

appliance tool, device, instrument, implement, utensil, gadget

appoint choose, name, assign, nominate

appreciate enjoy, value, respect, admire

appropriate suitable, fitting, proper inappropriate, unsuitable

approximately nearly, closely, roughly, about exactly

area region, district, section, location, territory, zone

argue disagree, quarrel, squabble, bicker agree

arid dry, waterless, parched wet

arm equip, fortify, empower disarm

army troops, forces, military

aroma odor, fragrance, scent

arrange organize, put in order, classify, sort

arrest stop, seize, apprehend, capture

arrive come, reach, get to, show up go

article 1. story, essay, report

article 2. item, thing, object

ashamed embarrassed, humiliated, mortified proud

ask request, question, inquire answer

assassinate kill, murder

assault attack, offense, onslaught

assemble 1. meet, gather together, congregate scatter

assemble 2. put together, set up, construct, build demolish, take apart

assignment task, chore, job, duty

assist help, aid, support, lend a hand hinder

assorted various, several, different, mixed

astonishing surprising, astounding, amazing

athletic sporting, gymnastic

attach fasten, join, connect, add detach

attack charge, bombard, ambush, storm, invade, raid

attempt try, undertake, endeavor, strive

attend go to, be present

attention care, consideration, concern, thoughtfulness

award

attract pull, interest, draw, lure repel

attractive lovely, pleasing, pretty, handsome unattractive, plain

author writer

autograph signature

average ordinary, usual, common unusual

award prize, reward

awful terrible, horrible, dreadful, atrocious pleasant

awkward clumsy, ungraceful, cumbersome, ungainly graceful

B

bald

baby infant, toddler

bad evil, naughty good

balance equalize, stabilize, steady

bald hairless, bare hairy

band orchestra

bandit robber, thief, gangster, highwayman, outlaw

bar 1. shut out, ban, block, exclude allow

bar 2. saloon, tavern

bare   uncovered, naked   covered
barely   scarcely, hardly
barter   trade, exchange, swap
bashful   shy, timid, modest, coy   bold
basic   fundamental, essential
bat   strike, hit, club
battle   fight, feud, war, struggle, combat, conflict
bawl   cry, weep
beach   shore, coast, seaside
beam   shine, glow
beast   animal, creature
beat   1. strike, hit, thrash, pound, pummel
beat   2. outdo, defeat, surpass, trounce
beautiful   attractive, lovely, pretty, handsome   ugly
before   earlier, previously, prior, formerly   after
beg   plead, implore
begin   start, commence, launch   end, conclude
behind   after, later than   ahead
believe   1. think, suppose, imagine, consider
believe   2. accept, trust   doubt
belly   stomach, abdomen
beneath   under, below   above
beneficial   helpful, useful, advantageous   harmful

bet   wager, gamble

between   among, betwixt

beyond   farther, past

big   1. large, huge, tremendous, enormous, immense   small

big   2. important, great, grand, considerable   unimportant

birth   beginning, origin, infancy   death, end

bitter   distasteful, unpleasant   pleasant, sweet

blade

blade   sword, knife

blame   accuse, charge, indict

blank   empty, vacant   filled

blast   explosion, blowout

bleak   dreary, dismal   cheerful

blend   mix, combine, join   separate

bless   praise, thank, glorify   curse

blind   sightless

blizzard   snowstorm

block   obstruct, hinder, check, restrain   permit

blockade   barrier, obstruction, barricade

bluff   deceive, trick, delude

board   mount, get on, embark   dismount, get off

boisterous   noisy, rowdy, shrill   quiet

bold   1. brave, courageous, fearless, gallant, heroic
cowardly

bold   2. arrogant, brazen, defiant, insolent   timid

bolt   1. run, flee, break away

bolt   2. lock, fastener

boring   dull, uninteresting   interesting

boss   1. supervise, oversee, direct

boss   2. manager, foreman, employer

bother   annoy, pester, disturb, irritate, harass, provoke

bottom   base, foundation, lowest part   top

bound   enclosed, surrounded

boundary   limit, border

box   1. fight, hit

box   2. crate, container

box (2)

brace   support, prop

brag   boast, crow, gloat

brake   stop, slow down, decelerate, curb   accelerate

branch   shoot, bough, limb

brand   kind, sort, type

brave   bold, courageous, fearless, gallant, heroic
cowardly

brawl   riot, racket, fracas

break   1. fracture, crack, crush, split, smash, shatter
mend, fix

branch

17

break 2. interruption, interval, intermission, pause, recess, rest

brief short, concise, terse long

bright 1. cheerful, sunny, shiny, vivid, sparkling, gleaming, glowing dull, dim

bright 2. smart, alert, intelligent dull

brilliant intelligent, wise stupid

bring carry, take, transport, deliver

broad wide, expansive narrow

bruise wound, injure, hurt

buddy friend, pal, companion, chum, partner

build make, create, construct, establish, form demolish

bulky broad, thick, lumpy narrow

bulletin message, newsletter

bumpy uneven, rocky, coarse smooth

bundle parcel, package

burglar thief, robber, housebreaker

burning

burning hot, fiery, sizzling, blazing, flaming

bury conceal, cover uncover

business work, occupation, profession, job

busy active, occupied, engaged idle

button fasten, clasp, close unbutton, open

buy purchase, shop sell

by   near, beside, at

C

cable   telegraph, wire
cafeteria   restaurant, snack bar, cafe
calculate   compute, count, figure, estimate
call   1. shout, yell
call   2. telephone
calm   quiet, still, peaceful, serene, tranquil
camouflage   disguise
campaign   crusade, movement, cause, drive
can   container, tin, receptacle
cancel   erase, wipe out, repeal
candidate   applicant, nominee
cap   top, cover, crown
capture   seize, arrest, catch, trap, apprehend   free, release
car   automobile, vehicle
care   1. thought, worry, attention, concern   neglect
care   2. protection, supervision, custody
careful   cautious, watchful   careless

can

carpet

chair

careless   sloppy, reckless, thoughtless   careful
carnival   fair, festival
carpet   rug, mat
carry   hold, transport, tote
carve   cut, slice
catalog   list, classify, group, sort
catastrophe   tragedy, disaster, calamity
catch   capture, seize, trap   release, free
cautious   careful, watchful, thoughtful   careless
cease   stop, end, halt, quit, conclude, discontinue
   continue
celebrate   1. proclaim, observe, commemorate
celebrate   2. rejoice
cemetery   graveyard
center   middle, heart, hub, core, nucleus
certain   sure, positive, definite   unsure
chair   seat, bench
challenge   dare, defy, confront
champion   winner, victor, best
chance   1. opportunity, occasion
chance   2. possibility, likelihood, prospect
chance   3. fate, luck
change   alter, modify, vary, switch   maintain
chapter   section, part, division

20

character 1. nature, temperament, makeup, disposition

character 2. role, part

charming appealing, pleasing, delightful unpleasant

chase 1. follow, run after, pursue

chase 2. drive away, repulse, reject

chat talk, gossip, discuss, converse

cheap inexpensive, low-priced expensive

cheat trick, deceive, swindle, defraud, dupe, bamboozle, mislead

check 1. restrain, curb, stop, control

check 2. prove, mark, verify

cheerful happy, glad, joyful, jolly, gay, merry sad, downcast

chest box, locker, safe

child youngster, kid adult

chilly cool, brisk, nippy warm

chisel sculpture, carve

choke strangle, suffocate, smother

choose pick, select, elect, opt

chop cut, cleave, sever, hack

chore task, job, work, assignment

chubby plump, fat, stout, stocky skinny

chubby

chuckle   giggle, laugh, titter

chum   friend, pal, companion, partner

city   metropolis, municipality

clamor   racket, ruckus, din, uproar, commotion
stillness, quiet

clean   spotless, spick-and-span   dirty

clear   1. remove, eliminate, rid

clear   2. bright, shining, vivid   muddy, dull

clever   smart, alert, bright, skillful, wise, sharp,
intelligent, quick-witted   dull

client   customer, patron

climate   weather

climb   mount, rise, ascend   descend

clip   1. cut, shear, crop, snip

clip   2. fasten, attach

1. close   1. shut, fasten, lock   open

close   2. end, finish, complete, conclude, stop   start

2. close   near, approaching   far

cloudy   dark, overcast, dismal   clear

club   1. group, association, clique

club (2)

club   2. bat, stick

club   3. strike, hit, knock

clue   sign, hint, evidence, lead

22

clumsy awkward, ungraceful, ungainly, gawky
graceful

coach train, tutor, teach

coarse 1. rough, uneven, bumpy, rocky, ragged
smooth

coarse 2. crude, vulgar, common refined

code laws, rules

cold chilly, frosty hot

collapse fall, topple

collect gather, accumulate, assemble scatter

colossal huge, gigantic, vast, immense, enormous,
mammoth tiny

combine join, unite, mix, blend, merge separate

comedian comic, funnyman

comfortable satisfied, contented, cozy, snug
uncomfortable

comical amusing, entertaining, funny, humorous,
witty

command order, direct, instruct

committee group, council, delegation

common 1. regular, ordinary, usual, familiar, everyday unusual, odd

common 2. coarse, crude, vulgar refined

commotion racket, ruckus, disturbance, tumult, confusion, fuss, excitement, clamor, hubbub, to-do
order, calmness

communicate inform, tell, enlighten

community district, area, town

companion friend, pal, chum, partner

company 1. business, firm, enterprise

company 2. guests, visitors

compare match, liken, contrast

complete 1. end, finish, conclude, wind up start

complete 2. whole, entire incomplete

complicated hard, involved, difficult, complex
simple

compliment praise, commend, flatter

conceal hide, cover, mask, camouflage disclose,
reveal

conceited vain, boastful, cocky, egotistical modest

concern 1. interest, care, worry

concern 2. business, company, firm

concert musical performance, recital

conclude end, finish, complete, close, stop open,
begin

condition circumstance, situation, state

1. conduct manage, direct, lead, guide

2. conduct behavior, manner

confident certain, sure, convinced, self-reliant
doubtful

24

confuse complicate, bewilder, dumfound, muddle, baffle, perplex, puzzle   clarify

congratulate compliment, commend, praise

connect join, unite, combine, link, attach   separate, disconnect

conquer overcome, overwhelm, overtake, overthrow, defeat, crush

consent permission, approval, acceptance, agreement   refusal

conserve keep, save, preserve   waste

consider think, study, ponder, contemplate, imagine

considerate thoughtful, kind, sympathetic, tactful   inconsiderate, unkind

console comfort, reassure, soothe

constantly continually, always

construct make, manufacture, build, form, create, assemble   demolish

consume eat, devour

contain hold, include, consist of, comprise

contented satisfied, pleased   discontented, dissatisfied

contest game, tournament, competition

continue persist, go on, keep on   discontinue, stop

control restrain, check, curb

convenient easy, handy, suitable   inconvenient

conversation talk, chat, discussion

convert change, transform

convict condemn, sentence clear, acquit

convince persuade

cool 1. chilly warm

cool 2. calm, unexcited excited

cooperate support, help, work together, collaborate hinder

copy imitate, duplicate, echo, repeat, reproduce

correct 1. right, true, accurate, proper, exact, appropriate incorrect, wrong

correct 2. improve, remedy

correspond write, communicate with

corridor hallway, passageway, aisle

counterfeit fake, imitation, copied real

country nation, land

courageous brave, bold, fearless, gallant, heroic cowardly

course line, track, direction

courteous polite, respectful, civil, gracious rude

cover 1. hide, conceal, protect, shelter uncover

cover 2. include, contain, consist of, comprise

cowardly timid, weak brave

coy timid, shy, modest, bashful bold

crack   break, split, fracture

crammed   stuffed, full, heaping, overflowing, loaded, packed, crowded, jammed

cranky   cross, annoyed, irritable, grouchy, disagreeable   pleasant

crazy   insane, mad, daft   sane

create   make, invent, originate, shape, form, manufacture, produce, design, establish

crew   team, gang, staff, force

crime   wrongdoing, sin, vice, evil

crook   criminal, gangster, lawbreaker

cross   cranky, annoyed, irritable, grouchy, disagreeable   pleasant

crowd   mob, throng, horde

cruel   mean, unkind, heartless, brutal, ruthless   kind

crush   press, squeeze, compress, squash

cry   weep, wail, sob, bawl

cuddle   snuggle, nestle

cure   heal, remedy

curious   inquisitive, nosy, prying, snoopy   uninterested

current   1. up-to-date, present, prevalent, new   old-fashioned

current   2. flow, stream

curse   swear, condemn

cry

27

curve   bend, wind, twist, turn

custom   way, manner, tradition, habit, practice

customer   client, buyer, patron

cut   1. snip, clip, slit, slash, saw, sever

cut   2. shorten, reduce, abbreviate, condense, abridge   increase

cute   attractive, bright, pretty   unattractive

D

dainty   delicate, fine, small   gross

damage   harm, hurt, impair, spoil   mend, fix

damp   moist, wet   dry

dangerous   unsafe, risky, hazardous   safe

daring   brave, bold, courageous, fearless, heroic   afraid, timid

dark   dim, gloomy, dismal, somber, dreary   bright

dart   dash, rush, hurry, scurry   dawdle

dash   dart, rush, hurry, scurry   dawdle

data   facts, information

date   appointment, engagement

dawdle   idle, loiter, linger, delay, tarry   hurry

dawn   daybreak, sunrise   dusk

dazzling   brilliant, shiny, glowing, glistening, blinding   dull

dead   lifeless, deceased, gone   alive

deal   agreement, understanding, bargain, transaction

debate   argue, dispute

deceive   cheat, trick, swindle, defraud, dupe, bamboozle, mislead

decent   proper, correct, suitable   improper

decide   settle, determine, resolve, judge

declare   say, state, exclaim, announce

decorate   beautify, trim, adorn

decorate

decrease   reduce, lessen, diminish, cut, shorten   increase

deduct   subtract, remove, withdraw   add

defeat   overcome, triumph, outdo, surpass

defend   protect, safeguard, shield, support   attack

define   explain, describe, clarify

definite   clear, precise, clear-cut, exact   unclear

deform   spoil, disfigure, mar

delay   postpone, put off, detain, stall

deliberately   purposely, intentionally, knowingly   accidentally

delicate   mild, fine, dainty, fragile   gross

delicious   luscious, tasty, appetizing   tasteless

delighted   happy, jubilant, overjoyed, elated   unhappy

delightful   pleasant, lovely, charming, appealing, pleasing   unpleasant

deliver   hand over, transfer

demand   ask, request

demolish   wreck, destroy, dismantle   restore

demon   devil, fiend, monster, ogre

demonstrate   show, display, present, exhibit, illustrate

depart

depart   leave, exit   arrive

dependable   trustworthy, reliable   undependable

deposit   place, put, leave   withdraw

depressed   sad, dejected, discouraged, downhearted, blue   happy

deprived   wanting, lacking, needing, missing, without

describe   define, portray, depict, characterize

desert   leave, forsake, abandon

deserve   earn, merit

design   draw, plan, sketch

desire   wish, want, long for

despise   hate, loathe, detest   love

destination   goal, end, objective

destroy   spoil, ruin, wreck   restore

detach   separate, unfasten, disconnect   attach

detest   despise, hate, loathe   love

detour   by-pass

develop   grow, mature, progress, advance, flourish

devil   demon, fiend, ogre, monster

devotion   1. love, affection, fondness

devotion   2. loyalty, dedication

devour   eat, consume

diagram   drawing, sketch, design

diary   account, record

die   pass away, perish, expire   live

different   unlike, distinct   same

difficult   hard, complicated, troublesome   easy

dig   scoop, excavate

dignified   noble, majestic, grand, distinguished
undignified

dim   dull, dark, faint, weak, indistinct   bright

dimension   measurement, size, proportions

dingy   dirty, dull, dark   bright

direct   1. show, point out, guide, lead, steer, escort

direct   2. manage, control, conduct, lead, head, guide,
command

detour

diary

dig

dirty

dirty   soiled, filthy   clean

disadvantage   drawback, handicap   advantage

disagree   differ, quarrel, dispute, argue, oppose   agree

disappear   vanish, fade away   appear

disaster   tragedy, calamity, misfortune, catastrophe

discard   throw away, reject, scrap   keep

discharge   dismiss, release, unload, dump

discipline   punish, correct, chastise

discouraged   depressed, dejected, downhearted   encouraged

discover   find, uncover, reveal, unearth

discuss   talk over

disease   sickness, illness, ailment, malady

disgrace   shame, embarrassment

disguise   conceal, mask, camouflage   reveal

disgusted   sickened, offended, nauseated, revolted

dishonest   untruthful, deceitful, crooked, untrustworthy   honest

dismal   dark, gloomy, dreary, bleak, depressing   bright

dismiss   discharge, expel, release

display   show, present, exhibit, demonstrate

dispute   argue, quarrel, fight   agree

distinct   plain, clear, obvious, exact, definite, clear-cut
unclear

distinguished   famous, honored, outstanding, cele-brated, dignified

distribute   dispense, allot, disperse   collect

district   area, region, section, neighborhood, zone

disturb   upset, annoy, bother

divide   separate, split   unite

divorce   separate, split   marry

dizzy   unsteady, confused, spinning   steady

dock   anchor, moor

doctor   physician, medic

document   certificate, statement

dodge   duck, avoid, evade

donate   contribute, give, present, grant

done   complete, finished, ended, concluded
unfinished

donkey   burro, ass

dose   portion, amount, quantity

doubt   question, mistrust, suspect   believe, trust

downfall   defeat, failure, ruin

downpour   rainstorm, cloudburst, flood

drab   dull, lifeless, flat, unattractive   bright,
attractive

dock

donkey

33

draft 1. wind, air current

draft 2. enlistment, enrollment, call-up, recruitment, induction

drag pull, tug, draw, haul, tow

drain empty, extract, draw off, remove fill

dramatize produce, present, stage

draw 1. sketch, portray, picture

draw 2. attract, lure repel

dreadful awful, terrible, horrible, vile, ghastly, wretched wonderful

dream imagine, fantasize

dreary gloomy, dull, dismal, dim, dark bright

drench soak, wet, flood, saturate

dress clothe, outfit, attire

drill practice, teach, train, exercise

drive steer, handle, operate

drizzle rain, shower, sprinkle

droop sag, drag, hang, dangle

drop end, cease, stop, let go, give up start, continue

drown sink, submerge, immerse

drowsy sleepy, dreamy alert

drug medicine, narcotic

drunk intoxicated, inebriated, tipsy sober

dry arid, parched wet

duck dodge, avoid, evade

dress

34

dull 1. dim, dark, faint, weak, indistinct bright

dull 2. stupid, slow, dim-witted, dumb smart

dull 3. boring, uninteresting, monotonous interesting

dumb 1. stupid, dull, dim-witted smart

dumb 2. speechless, mute, silent

dummy 1. imitation, copy, model

dummy 2. dope, dolt, dunce, fool

dump empty, unload, discard, scrap, throw away load

dunce dummy, dope, dolt, fool

duplicate copy, repeat, reproduce, double

dusk sunset, sundown, evening, nightfall dawn

duty task, job, chore, work, assignment, obligation, responsibility

dye color, stain, tint

dynamic active, energetic, forceful, intense weak

E

eager anxious, enthusiastic

earn deserve, merit, gain

earth (2)

earth 1. soil, dirt, ground

earth 2. world, globe

easy simple, plain, uncomplicated hard

eat dine, consume

echo reflect, resound, reverberate

eclipse blackout, shadow

edge border, frame, rim

edit correct, check, rewrite, revise, amend

educate teach, train, tutor, instruct, enlighten

eerie weird, spooky, strange, ghostly

effort try, attempt, undertaking, endeavor

elastic flexible, springy, stretchable inflexible

elder older, senior younger

elect pick, select, choose

elegant refined, tasteful, polished common, vulgar

elementary basic, beginning, introductory, fundamental, primary advanced

elevate lift, raise, boost, hoist lower

eligible qualified, fit, suitable ineligible

eliminate discard, remove, throw out, reject, exclude
include

else other, different

embarrassed ashamed, humiliated, mortified

embrace grasp, hug, hold, clutch

emergency crisis, pinch

emotion   feeling, sentiment

emphasize   stress, accent, highlight

employ   hire, sign up, engage   fire

empty   blank, vacant, hollow, barren   full

enclosed   surrounded, fenced, contained, restricted, encircled   open

encourage   urge, nudge, prod, support, inspire   discourage

end   finish, stop, cease, complete, conclude, terminate, discontinue, quit   begin

endless   constant, continuous, nonstop, infinite

enemy   foe, opponent, opposition   friend

energy   strength, force, power, might, vitality, pep, vigor

engrave   print, inscribe, stamp, carve

enjoy   like, admire, relish   dislike

enlarge   expand, inflate, increase, amplify, magnify   reduce, shrink

enlist   enroll, register, sign up, join

enormous   huge, giant, immense, vast, gigantic, colossal   tiny

enough   plenty, sufficient, ample, adequate   insufficient

enraged   angry, mad, furious, provoked

enroll   enlist, register, join, sign up

entertaining   interesting, amusing, fascinating, absorbing, delightful   boring, dull

enthusiastic eager, interested indifferent

entire whole, full, complete, total partial

envious jealous

environment neighborhood, surroundings

equal tie, match, parallel

equip provide, furnish, supply, outfit

erase rub out, cancel

erect build, construct

errand task, job, assignment, chore

escape flee, get away

escort accompany, chaperone

essay composition, article, paper

essential important, needed, necessary, vital
  unimportant

establish create, set up, organize, form

estimate figure, judge, guess, compute, calculate

etiquette manners, rules of conduct, amenities

evaporate fade away, disappear, vanish

even 1. level, flat, smooth uneven

even 2. same, equal, identical different

evening sunset, sundown, dusk, nightfall morning

event incident, happening, experience, occurrence

eventually finally, in time, ultimately

evict expel, oust, turn out

evidence facts, proof, signs, clues

evil bad, sinful, wicked good

exactly precisely

exaggerate magnify, stretch, overstate minimize

examine 1. inspect, study, observe

examine 2. test, quiz, question

example sample, model, specimen

excellent very good, fine, splendid, superb inferior

except excluding, besides, barring including

exceptional notable, outstanding, unusual, extraordinary, remarkable ordinary

exchange trade, change, substitute, switch, swap

excited enthusiastic, eager, interested indifferent

excursion trip, journey, tour, outing

1. excuse reason, alibi

2. excuse pardon, forgive, absolve blame

executive administrator, manager, director, officer

exercise practice, drill, train, prepare, condition

exercise

exhausted tired, weary, fatigued energetic

exhibit show, display, present, demonstrate

exile banish, expel, deport

exit depart, go out, leave enter

expand spread, grow, enlarge, increase, broaden contract, reduce

expect look for, await, anticipate

expedition journey, trip, pilgrimage

expel remove, discharge, dismiss, oust admit

expensive costly, high-priced, dear cheap

experience event, incident, happening, occurrence

experiment try, test

expired ended, ceased, discontinued

explain clarify, describe, simplify

explode burst, blow up

explore search, research, investigate, probe

express 1. fast, quick, speedy, rapid, swift slow

express 2. present, tell, describe

exquisite beautiful, gorgeous, stunning, dazzling ugly

extend increase, enlarge, stretch, lengthen, expand, broaden reduce, decrease

exterminate destroy, get rid of, eliminate, kill, wipe out

extinct dead, gone, obsolete

extinguish put out, smother, crush

extra additional, more, spare, surplus

extraordinary special, unusual, remarkable, exceptional, noteworthy, memorable ordinary

extreme exaggerated, overdone, extravagant moderate

F

fable   story, fairy tale, legend, myth

fabric   cloth, material

fabulous   wonderful, marvelous, splendid, superb, spectacular, remarkable

face   meet, confront, encounter

fact   detail, item, point

factory   plant

fabric

fad   style, fashion, craze, rage

fade   dim, lose color, weaken

fail   flop, flunk, be unsuccessful succeed

faint   1. weak, dim, faded, pale, dull, hazy strong, bright

faint   2. black out, swoon, weaken

fair   1. right, correct, just, honest, impartial unfair, unjust

fair   2. sunny, clear, pleasant, bright cloudy

fair   3. average, mediocre

fair   4. light, pale dark

fair   5. festival, bazaar

fall (1)

fairy   elf, pixie, sprite

faith   1. trust, hope, belief, confidence

faith   2. religion, teaching

fake   imitation, false, counterfeit   real

fall   1. drop, descend, tumble, topple, plunge, collapse   rise

fall   2. autumn

false   1. wrong, incorrect, untrue   true

false   2. fake, counterfeit   real

familiar   popular, well-known, common   strange

family   group, kin, relatives, folks

famous   popular, well-known, celebrated, renowned

fan   admirer, follower

fancy   elaborate, frilly, flowery, fussy, ornate   simple, plain

fantastic   incredible, unusual, extraordinary, exceptional, remarkable, wonderful, marvelous   ordinary

far   distant, remote, removed   near

fare   charge, toll, fee

farm   grow, raise, harvest, cultivate

fascinating   interesting, absorbing, exciting, thrilling, captivating   boring

fashion   1. make, form, shape, create, mold

fashion   2. style, mode, vogue

fast   rapid, swift, speedy, quick   slow

farm

fasten   secure, tie, bind, attach, close, seal   untie, open

fat   heavy, stout, plump, chubby   thin

faucet   spigot, tap

fault   mistake, error

favor   good deed, kindness, service

favorite   best, choice, prized, pet

fear   fright, dread, alarm, panic, terror

fearless   brave, daring, bold, courageous, heroic   afraid

feast   banquet, treat

fee   charge, fare, toll, dues

feeble   weak, frail   strong

feed   nourish, supply, nurture

feel   touch, handle, finger

female   feminine, womanly   male

fence   1. enclosure, wall, barrier

fence   2. fight, duel, joust

ferocious   fierce, savage, vicious, brutal, cruel, wild, ruthless   tame

fertile   fruitful, rich, productive   barren

feud   fight, disagree, argue, dispute, quarrel, battle

fib   lie, untruth, falsehood

field   land, tract, plot

fiend   devil, demon, monster, ogre

fierce   ferocious, violent, raging, savage, wild, vicious
   gentle

fiery   hot, burning, flaming

fight   dispute, feud, battle, struggle

figure   shape, form, build, physique

file   1. sort, classify, group, categorize

file   2. grind, smooth, sand, sharpen

fill   load, pack, stuff, supply   empty

filter   strain, screen, sift, separate

filthy   dirty, grimy, polluted   clean

final   last, closing, concluding   beginning

finale   end, conclusion, finish   opening

find   discover, detect, learn, uncover, disclose   lose

fine   1. good, excellent, splendid

fine   2. delicate, dainty   rough

fine   3. penalize, charge, tax

finish   end, conclude, complete, close, stop   start

fire   1. blaze, flame

fire   2. dismiss, discharge, lay off   hire

fire   3. shoot, discharge, blast

firm   1. hard, solid, rigid, inflexible, immovable
   flexible

firm   2. company, business, enterprise

fit   1. healthy, strong, well   unfit

fit   2. attack, seizure, spell, convulsion

fix   repair, mend, adjust, regulate   break
flag   pennant, banner, standard
flame   fire, blaze
flat   smooth, even, level   uneven
flatter   praise, compliment
flee   run away, bolt, escape
flexible   elastic, springy, stretchable, pliable   rigid, inflexible
flimsy   weak, fragile   strong, sturdy
fling   toss, hurl, pitch, throw
flood   overfill, drench, overflow
floor   1. ground, pavement
floor   2. level, story
flower   blossom, bloom, develop, flourish
fluid   liquid, flowing, watery   solid
fly   soar, glide
foe   enemy, opponent   friend
foggy   cloudy, dim, smoky, misty   clear
fold   bend, double over, crease   unfold
follow   1. chase, trail, track, pursue
follow   2. obey, use, practice
fondness   liking, love, affection
foolish   silly, stupid, dumb, ridiculous, senseless
forbid   prohibit, bar, ban, prevent   allow

flag

fling

force 1. compel, make, drive, pressure, push

force 2. power, strength, energy

forecast prediction, prophecy

forgive pardon, excuse, absolve blame

forlorn sad, hopeless, melancholy, unhappy, downcast, despondent cheerful

form make, develop, shape, fashion, create, construct, mold

fortunate lucky unlucky

forward onward, ahead backward

foundation 1. base, ground

foundation 2. establishment, organization, institution

fraction part, portion, segment

fracture break, crack, shatter, smash, split, rupture heal

frail weak, slight, delicate, fragile strong

frame border, edge, trim

frantic excited, hysterical, upset, frenzied calm

freak unusual, queer, grotesque, bizarre

free 1. release, clear, dismiss, discharge, liberate, acquit, emancipate restrain

free 2. complimentary, gratis

frequently often, regularly, repeatedly seldom

friend companion, buddy, pal enemy

frame

46

frighten   scare, alarm, terrify

frosting   icing, topping

frosty   icy, cold   hot

frown   pout, scowl   smile

full   packed, heaping, overflowing, loaded, stuffed, crowded, jammed, crammed   empty

fun   pleasure, entertainment, enjoyment

funny   amusing, entertaining, humorous, comical, laughable   sad

fur   pelt, hide, skin

furious   angry, annoyed, enraged, mad, infuriated   calm

furnish   supply, provide, equip, outfit

fuse   unite, join, combine, weld   separate

fuss   commotion, uproar, racket, riot, to-do, excitement

G

gadget   contraption, tool, device, appliance

gallant   brave, bold, courageous, fearless, heroic   cowardly

gate

gem

gamble bet, wager, risk

gang group, crew, ring, crowd, mob, band

gap opening, hole, space

garbage rubbish, trash, waste, junk, refuse

garden plant, grow, raise, cultivate

gash cut, wound, laceration

gate fence, barrier

gather collect, assemble, accumulate, amass, compile
  scatter

gay 1. happy, lively, jolly, cheerful, jovial, vivacious
  glum

gay 2. colorful, bright, vivid dull

gaze stare, gape, gawk

gem jewel, precious stone, treasure

general officer, commander

generous giving, unselfish, kind, bighearted, liberal
  selfish, stingy

gentle soft, mild, tender, soothing harsh, rough

genuine real, true, pure, authentic fake

ghost spirit, phantom, spook

giant colossal, huge, gigantic, vast, immense, enormous, mammoth tiny

gift 1. present, offering

gift 2. talent, ability, forte

48

gigantic   colossal, huge, giant, vast, immense, enormous, mammoth   tiny

giggle   laugh, chuckle, snicker

give   present, hand over, provide, supply   take

glacier   iceberg

glad   happy, pleased, cheerful, delighted, joyful, satisfied   unhappy

glamorous   beautiful, attractive, stunning, gorgeous, dazzling   unattractive

glance   look, glimpse

glare   stare, scowl

glaring   bright, shining, glowing, flashing, dazzling, blinding   dim

gleaming   bright, shining, glowing, beaming, sparkling   dim

glide   move easily, slide, skim, coast

globe   sphere, earth, world, universe

gloomy   dark, dismal, dim, dreary, depressing, glum, bleak   cheerful

glorious   great, grand, magnificent, splendid, superb, majestic, wonderful, divine, sensational, marvelous

glowing   bright, shining, gleaming, beaming, sparkling   dim

glue

glue   paste, cement, stick together

glum   sad, gloomy, depressed, moody   cheerful

goal   aim, object, target, purpose

gobble   gulp, eat fast, devour

good   fine, nice, proper, right, appropriate, decent
bad

gorgeous   beautiful, stunning, glorious, dazzling, ravishing   ugly

govern   rule, control, regulate, command, manage, head, lead, supervise, direct, run

grab   snatch, seize, grasp, clutch

gracious   polite, pleasant, kindly, courteous, cordial, friendly   rude, unkind

grade   1. mark, score

grade   2. class, division, group, category

graduate   pass, succeed, advance

grand   great, stately, majestic, magnificent, glorious, splendid

grant   1. give, donate, contribute, present, award

grant   2. let, allow, permit   deny

grasp   grab, snatch, seize, clutch, grip, hold   release

grateful   thankful, appreciative   ungrateful

grave   burial place, plot

grease   oil, fat, lubrication

great   grand, magnificent, glorious, splendid, superb, majestic, wonderful, sensational

grimy   dirty, filthy, soiled   clean

grin   smile, smirk

grind crush, mash, crumble, squash, pulverize

grip grasp, hold, seize, clutch

gross crude, coarse, vulgar, unrefined refined

grotesque deformed, monstrous, disfigured, ugly, bizarre

grouchy annoyed, cranky, cross, irritable, disagreeable, crabby, grumpy, moody pleasant, cheerful

group sort, classify, arrange, organize

grow 1. develop, mature, age, progress, increase shrink

grow 2. plant, raise, cultivate

growl snarl, grumble, complain

guarantee promise, assure, pledge

guard watch, protect, defend, shield, secure, patrol

guard

guess think, believe, suppose, assume, imagine

guest visitor, company

guide 1. show, direct, point out, lead, steer, escort

guide 2. manage, direct, control, regulate, advise, conduct

guilty criminal, to blame, at fault innocent

gun weapon, firearm, pistol, revolver

gun

gymnastics exercises, athletics, acrobatics, calisthenics

gyp cheat, trick, deceive, swindle, defraud, dupe, bamboozle, mislead

H

hammer (2)

habit   custom, practice, pattern, routine

hall   1. corridor, passageway, vestibule

hall   2. meeting room, auditorium

halt   stop, end, conclude, quit   start

hammer   1. pound, hit, knock, bang

hammer   2. mallet

hand   give, turn over, deliver, pass, transfer

handbag   purse, pocketbook

handicap   burden, disadvantage

handle   1. feel, touch, finger, manipulate

handle   2. manage, direct, carry on, run

handsome   good-looking, attractive   ugly

handy   1. useful, nearby, ready, available, convenient   inconvenient

handy   2. skilled, expert, clever, apt, adept   clumsy, inept

happen   occur, take place

happy   glad, cheerful, contented, joyful, jolly, gay, pleased, satisfied   unhappy, sad

52

harbor   port, dock, pier, wharf

hard   1. firm, solid, stiff, rigid   soft

hard   2. difficult, tough, rough   easy

hardly   barely, scarcely, nearly

hardy   strong, tough, healthy, sturdy, rugged, robust   weak

harm   hurt, damage, injure, impair

harsh   cruel, severe, gruff, hard, rough, stern, tough, curt, brusque   kind

harvest   crop, produce, output, yield

hasty   1. quick, fast, swift, rapid, speedy, hurried   slow

hasty   2. rash, reckless, impulsive

hatch   produce, breed, generate

hate   detest, despise, loathe   love

haul   drag, pull, tug, tow

haunted   spooky, weird, eerie, possessed

hazardous   dangerous, unsafe, risky   safe

hazy   1. dim, cloudy, misty, overcast, foggy   clear

hazy   2. unclear, vague, fuzzy, uncertain, confused   clear

head   lead, supervise, command, direct, manage, control, conduct, run

heading   title, headline

heal   cure, remedy, correct, mend, repair

heaping   full, overflowing, loaded, piled, stuffed, stacked

heavy   fat, stout, plump, hefty   thin

hectic   busy, exciting, frantic   calm

help   aid, assist, cooperate, support   hinder

hem   border, edge, rim

heroic   brave, bold, courageous, fearless, gallant   cowardly

hide   conceal, cover, mask, camouflage   reveal

hideous   ugly, horrible, dreadful, awful, ghastly, wretched   beautiful

high

high   tall, towering, elevated   low

highway   road, turnpike, expressway, thruway

hilarious   funny, humorous, laughable, comical

hint   clue, suggestion

hire   1. employ, engage   fire

hire   2. lease, rent, charter

hit   strike, bat, slap, smack, slug, swat

hoist   raise, lift, boost, elevate   lower

hole   gap, opening, cavity

hollow   empty, vacant

home   residence, dwelling

homely   ugly, plain, unattractive   attractive

honest truthful, upright, moral, ethical, honorable, sincere dishonest

hook fasten, clip, latch, clasp, snap unhook

horrible dreadful, awful, terrible, frightful, ghastly, wretched

hot 1. steaming, sweltering, sizzling, torrid cold

hot 2. spicy, sharp, peppery, tangy bland

house shelter, home, residence, dwelling

house

howl cry, yell, shout, scream, screech, roar, wail

hubbub noise, racket, commotion, disturbance, tumult, confusion, fuss, excitement, clamor, to-do stillness, calm

huddle crowd, gather, cluster, assemble

hug embrace, grasp, hold, clutch, squeeze

huge gigantic, colossal, giant, vast, immense, enormous, mammoth tiny

humble modest, plain, simple, unpretentious showy

humid moist, damp, muggy dry

humiliated embarrassed, ashamed, mortified

humorous funny, laughable, comical, witty

hunger appetite, craving, desire

hunt seek, search, look, scout

hurl toss, fling, throw, pitch

hurry rush, hasten, speed, dash, hustle

hut

hurt   harm, damage, injure, impair

husband   spouse, mate, married man

husky   sturdy, rugged, muscular, strong, athletic   slight

hut   cabin, shed, shanty, shack

hypnotize   entrance, spellbind, mesmerize

hysterical   upset, uncontrollable, frantic, overexcited, delirious   calm

I

icing

icing   frosting, topping

idea   thought, notion, concept

identify   name, describe, label, tag

idiot   imbecile, moron, half-wit, fool, simpleton

ignore   avoid, snub, overlook

ill   sick, ailing   healthy

illegal   unlawful, criminal   legal

illustrate   picture, draw, portray

imagine   1. think, guess, suppose, believe

imagine   2. dream, fantasize, envision

56

imbecile   idiot, moron, half-wit, fool, simpleton

imitate   copy, repeat, duplicate

immediately   now, instantly, at once, promptly   later

immense   huge, giant, enormous, vast, gigantic, colossal   tiny

impatient   restless, edgy   patient

impolite   rude, disrespectful, ill-mannered, insolent   polite

important   necessary, meaningful, significant, urgent, major   unimportant

impossible   unthinkable, absurd   possible

improve   better, perfect, advance

incident   event, happening, occurrence

incinerator   furnace, burner

include   contain, cover   exclude

income   earnings, wages, pay, salary

incomplete   unfinished, partial   complete

inconsiderate   thoughtless, unkind   considerate, thoughtful

incorrect   wrong, inaccurate, faulty, mistaken   right, correct

increase   enlarge, expand, extend, inflate   decrease

incredible   unbelievable, absurd, fantastic

independent   1. acting alone, self-reliant   dependent

independent   2. neutral, impartial

indicate show, point out, demonstrate, express, signify

indistinct unclear, vague, cloudy, dim, hazy, blurred clear

inexpensive cheap, low-priced, reasonable expensive

infect contaminate, pollute, poison

inflate expand, stretch deflate

inflexible firm, rigid, stiff flexible

influence move, sway, persuade

inform tell, notify, report, instruct

information news, facts, knowledge, data

infuriate anger, upset, enrage, irritate, provoke soothe

ingredient part, element, factor, component

injure harm, hurt, damage, impair

inn lodge, hotel, motel

innocent blameless, without guilt guilty

inquire ask, question, investigate

inquisitive curious, snooping, nosy

insane crazy, mad, unbalanced sane

insignia emblems, symbols, badges

insist urge, press, demand, push

inspect examine, observe, study, review

inn

inspire   influence, encourage

instantly   immediately, fast, promptly, quickly, rapidly, swiftly

institution   organization, establishment

instruct   teach, show, educate, inform, tell, advise

instrument   tool, device, implement, utensil, gadget, appliance

insult   offend, affront

intelligent   bright, smart, alert, wise   ignorant

interesting   entertaining, amusing, fascinating, absorbing, captivating   boring, uninteresting

interfere   intrude, meddle

intermission   recess, pause, break, interval

interpret   explain, clarify

interrupt   break in, interfere, intrude

interview   question, quiz, interrogate

intrude   interfere, meddle

invade   raid, attack, overrun

invalid   sickly, weak, unhealthy, frail   healthy

invent   make up, develop, originate, create, produce, discover, devise

investigate   look into, explore, examine, inspect, study, probe

invite   ask, call

irritable   cross, cranky, annoyed, grouchy, disagreeable   pleasant

irritate 1. annoy, bother, anger, infuriate, provoke

irritate 2. rub, chafe, inflame soothe

issue 1. topic, subject, theme, question, point

issue 2. copy, edition

J

jab poke, push, thrust

jail lock up, imprison, incarcerate

jam 1. crowd, stuff, cram, squeeze, crush, load

jam 2. jelly, marmalade, preserve

jealous envious

jewel gem, stone

job work, employment, task, assignment, duty, occupation, position

jog

jog run, sprint

join connect, unite, combine, link, attach separate,
detach

jolly merry, cheerful, jovial, gay, happy, pleasant
glum

journey expedition, trip, excursion, pilgrimage

joyful jolly, merry, cheerful, jovial, gay, happy glum
judge referee, umpire, mediator
jumble mix, scramble
jumbo gigantic, colossal, huge, giant, immense, enormous tiny
jump spring, leap, bound
junk rubbish, trash, scrap
just fair, proper, moral unjust
juvenile young, youthful old

jump

K

keep save, preserve, conserve discard
kennel doghouse, pound
key 1. clue, hint, evidence, lead, explanation
key 2. pitch, tone, note
kid 1. tease, fool, joke, jest
kid 2. child, tot
kidnap snatch, abduct
kill slay, murder, slaughter, execute, assassinate
kind 1. considerate, thoughtful, sympathetic, gentle, helpful unkind, mean

kid (2)

knife

kind 2. sort, type, variety

king ruler, chief, monarch, sovereign

kit equipment, set, furnishings, gear

knife blade, sword

knock hit, strike, beat, hammer, rap, bang

L

label tag, name, title

labor work, toil

lack want, need, require

ladle dipper, scoop

land arrive, touch down, descend

lane path, road, aisle

large big, huge, tremendous, enormous, immense, grand, massive small

lariat rope, lasso

lasso rope, lariat

last final, end first, beginning

latch lock, hook, clasp, fastener

lariat

laugh giggle, chuckle

launch start, begin, introduce, establish

law rule, regulation, principle, act, ordinance

lay put, place, set

lazy lax, idle, inactive active

lead guide, conduct, manage, direct, head

league union, group, alliance

leap jump, spring, bound

learn 1. find out, discover

learn 2. memorize

lease rent, hire, charter

leash strap, chain

least fewest, smallest, minimum most

leave 1. go, depart, exit arrive

leave 2. quit, abandon, desert stay

lecture speech, talk, address

ledge shelf, edge

ledge

legal lawful, permitted, allowed, legitimate, author-ized illegal

legend story, tale, fable, myth

lend give, loan borrow

lengthen extend, stretch, prolong shorten

less fewer, smaller more

lesson assignment, exercise

letter

let permit, allow, consent

letter message, note, dispatch

level flat, even, smooth uneven

liberty freedom, independence, emancipation

license permission, consent, approval, authorization

lid cover, top, cap

lie fib, exaggerate

lift hoist, raise, boost, elevate lower

light 1. bright, clear dark

light 2. weightless, airy, delicate heavy

like enjoy, admire, appreciate dislike

limit end, boundary, restriction

link join, connect, unite, combine, attach, bridge separate

liquid fluid solid

list record, enumerate

litter rubbish, scrap, junk, trash, garbage

little small, tiny, minute, slight big

live dwell, reside

lively active, energetic, animated, vivacious, spry, spirited, gay dull

load 1. burden, cargo, freight

load 2. fill, stuff, pack unload

loaf   idle, lounge, loiter

loan   give, lend

lobby   entrance, vestibule

location   area, place, site, spot, region

lock   fasten, close, hook, clasp, latch, shut   unlock, open

lock

logical   reasonable, sensible, rational   unreasonable

lonely   alone, friendless, isolated

look   1. see, glance, gaze, stare

look   2. seem, appear

loose   slack, limp, drooping   tight

lose   1. fail, flop, be unsuccessful   win

lose   2. misplace, mislay   find

lottery   raffle, drawing

loud   noisy, thunderous, roaring   soft

love   adore, idolize, cherish, admire   hate

lovely   attractive, pleasing, pretty, delightful, charming, appealing, beautiful   unattractive

loyal   faithful, true, devoted, trustworthy   disloyal

lucky   fortunate   unlucky

luggage   baggage, bags, suitcases, valises

luggage

luxurious   extravagant, elegant, magnificent, grand, splendid

M

maid

mail (2)

mad 1. crazy, insane, deranged sane

mad 2. angry, furious, enraged, annoyed, cross, irritated

magazine periodical, journal

magic witchcraft, voodoo, wizardry, sorcery

magnetic attractive, pulling, drawing

magnificent grand, great, stately, majestic, glorious, splendid, superb, exquisite, marvelous, wonderful

magnify enlarge, expand, exaggerate, stretch, inflate, increase, amplify minimize

maid servant, housekeeper, domestic

mail 1. send, dispatch

mail 2. letters, correspondence

main chief, principal, foremost, leading

make 1. build, construct, create, manufacture, produce, form, assemble

make 2. force, cause, compel

make 3. kind, type, sort, brand

manage conduct, direct, lead, guide, run, operate, control, govern, supervise

manner way, style, nature, character, method

manual guidebook, handbook, directory

manufacture make, build, construct, create, produce, form, assemble

map

many numerous, various, several few

map chart

marathon race, contest

march walk, hike, parade

margin border, edge, rim

marionette puppet, doll

mark grade, rating

market store, shop, mart

marvelous wonderful, extraordinary, glorious, great, grand, magnificent, splendid, superb, divine, sensational, spectacular ordinary

marionette

mash crush, crumble, grind, pulverize

mask disguise, camouflage

masquerade disguise, pretend, pose, impersonate

master head, chief, ruler, commander

match contest, game, battle

mature full-grown, adult, developed, ripe immature

maximum most, greatest, largest minimum

maybe perhaps, possibly

67

meadow

meadow   pasture, field, grassland

mean   1. suggest, signify, imply

mean   2. unkind, cross, irritable, malicious   kind

mechanic   repairman, technician

medal   award, prize, honor, medallion

medicine   drug, cure, remedy

meek   shy, timid, gentle, tame, mild, modest   aggressive

meet   assemble, gather, congregate, unite

melody   tune, song

melt   soften, dissolve

mend   fix, repair, adjust, regulate   break

merchandise   goods, products, wares

merchant   storekeeper, dealer

merge   combine, unite, mix, blend, join, fuse   separate

merry   gay, happy, lively, jolly, cheerful, jovial   glum

message   word, report, communication, dispatch

messy   sloppy, careless, untidy, dirty   neat

meter   gauge, measure

method   plan, manner, means, system, way, style, procedure

microscopic   tiny, minute   huge

middle   center, heart, core, hub

mighty   strong, powerful, great, grand   weak

mild   gentle, calm, moderate   harsh

military army, troops, soldiers, armed forces

mimic copy, imitate, mock, mime, ape

mind 1. brain, intellect

mind 2. watch, tend, look after

miniature small, tiny, minute giant

minimum least, smallest maximum

minister clergyman, pastor, chaplain

1. minute instant, moment

2. minute tiny, small, miniature giant

miraculous remarkable, wonderful, marvelous, extraordinary, incredible

mischievous naughty, devilish, playful

miserable 1. sad, unhappy, downcast happy

miserable 2. wretched, mean pleasant

misfortune trouble, difficulty, mishap, sorrow

mislead deceive, trick, dupe

misplace lose, mislay

missile rocket, projectile

missile

missing lost, absent, gone present

mission job, errand, task, assignment, chore, duty

mistake error, fault, slip, blunder, oversight

mistreat abuse, molest, manhandle

misty cloudy, foggy, smoky clear

69

misunderstanding difficulty, difference, disagreement

mix blend, combine, join, stir, scramble separate

moan groan, complain, wail

mob crowd, throng, horde

model duplicate, reproduction, likeness, replica

modern new, up-to-date, advanced, contemporary, recent old-fashioned

modest humble, bashful, shy, quiet bold

moist damp, wet, soggy dry

mold 1. shape, form, carve, sculpture

mold 2. decay, rot, spoil

molest harm, mistreat, annoy, abuse

moment instant, minute

monarch ruler, king, sovereign

money currency, cash

monitor helper, assistant

monotonous boring, dull, tedious, humdrum interesting

monster fiend, ogre, demon, freak

mood feeling, temperament, disposition

moody gloomy, glum, depressed, temperamental, sullen

mop scrub, swab

money

70

motion movement, activity
mountain hill, elevation
movement motion, activity
mow cut, clip, crop, shear
mud slime, dirt, muck
muggy humid, damp, sticky, dank
murder kill, slay, slaughter, execute, assassinate
mutiny rebellion, revolt, riot, uprising
mystery puzzle, problem
myth fable, story, fairy tale, legend

mow

N

nag pester, annoy, bother
nail fasten, attach, fix, secure
naked uncovered, undressed, nude, bare covered
name label, tag, title
nap sleep, doze, drowse, snooze
narcotics drugs, opiates
narrator storyteller
narrow cramped, confined, limited, restricted, close, tight wide

nap

71

nasty   unpleasant, disgusting, repulsive, offensive, obnoxious   pleasant, delightful

nation   country, land

natural   genuine, real, pure   artificial

naturally   certainly, surely, of course

naughty   bad, disobedient, mischievous   good, obedient

near   close, at hand   far

nearly   almost, close to

neat   tidy, orderly, well-kept   sloppy, messy

necessary   needed, important, essential, urgent, required   unnecessary

need   want, lack, require

neglected   overlooked, ignored, slighted   protected

neighborhood   area, surroundings, vicinity, environment

nerve   courage, daring

nervous   restless, upset, disturbed, shaken, flustered, tense, edgy, jittery   calm

new   modern, current, up-to-date, recent   old

nice   pleasant, agreeable, good, fine   unpleasant

noise   racket, clamor, commotion, uproar   quiet

nominate   name, select, choose, designate

nonsense   foolishness, stupidity, rubbish, bunk

normal   regular, usual, typical, standard, ordinary
unusual, abnormal

nosy   snoopy, curious, prying

note   memo, message

notice   see, observe, note

notify   tell, report, advise, inform

now   immediately, instantly, at once, promptly, presently   later

nudge   encourage, urge, prod, push, prompt, inspire

nuisance   pest, annoyance

numb   unfeeling, deadened

number   1. quantity, count, amount

number   2. numeral, figure, symbol, digit

numeral   number, figure, symbol, digit

numerous   many, a lot, several, various   few

nurse   care for, tend to, nurture

nutrition   food, nourishment

note

oath   pledge, promise, vow

obey   listen to, mind, comply   disobey

1. object   1. thing, article, item

  object   2. goal, purpose, aim, target

2. object   complain, protest, disagree, challenge, disapprove   approve, agree

obnoxious   nasty, unpleasant, disgusting, hateful, disagreeable, repulsive, offensive   pleasant, agreeable

observe   see, look, watch, study, examine

obstacle   barrier, block, snag, obstruction

obstinate   stubborn, willful, headstrong, pigheaded, ornery   flexible

obstruction   obstacle, barrier, block, snag

obtain   get, receive, gain, acquire

obvious   plain, clear, evident, apparent   vague, unclear

occupation   business, work, job, profession, employment, trade

occur   happen, take place, transpire

odd   strange, unusual, peculiar, queer, weird, bizarre   ordinary

odor   smell, scent, aroma, fragrance

office   1. workplace, studio, headquarters

office   2. position, post, role

often   many times, frequently, repeatedly   seldom

ogre   monster, fiend, demon

old   aged, elderly   young

omit   leave out, miss, skip, exclude   include

only   just, simply, merely

ooze   seep, leak

open   start, begin, launch, establish   close

operate   work, run, manage, handle

opinion   belief, judgment, feeling, sentiment, attitude, view, thought

old

opponent   enemy, competitor, rival, adversary   ally

opportunity   chance, occasion

oppose   fight, disagree, argue, dispute, quarrel, contradict, resist   agree

optimistic   hopeful, cheerful, bright, lighthearted, carefree   pessimistic

oral   spoken, voiced, verbal

orbit   path, circuit, circle, revolution

order   1. arrangement, manner, system

order   2. command, instruction, directive

ordinary   usual, common, normal, average, everyday   unusual

organize   set up, arrange, classify, systematize, categorize

ornament

original 1. firsthand, authentic copied

original 2. novel, new, fresh, different, unique ordinary

ornament decoration, trimming, adornment

ornery 1. stubborn, obstinate, willful, headstrong, pigheaded flexible

ornery 2. mean, cranky, grouchy, cross, difficult pleasant, agreeable

outcome result, effect, end, conclusion, consequence

outfit equip, provide, furnish, supply

outing trip, journey, tour, jaunt, excursion

outline plan, sketch, diagram, draft

outlook view, attitude, position

outrageous absurd, unbelievable, ridiculous, shocking, extreme, ludicrous ordinary, sensible

outstanding important, well-known, great, distinguished, famous, celebrated, prominent ordinary, unimportant

overcast cloudy, dark, dismal clear

overcome conquer, defeat, upset, overpower, surmount surrender, yield

overlook ignore, neglect, disregard, skip, miss

overpass bridge, span, viaduct

oversight error, slip, omission

overthrow defeat, overcome, overpower, destroy, upset

own have, possess

P

pace rate, speed

pack fill, load, stuff empty

pact agreement, understanding, treaty

pad 1. notebook, tablet

pad 2. pillow, cushion

pageant show, exhibition, parade, display, review, spectacle

pail bucket

pain ache, hurt, discomfort, soreness, pang

paint 1. coat, color, cover

paint 2. picture, draw, illustrate, portray, depict

pair set, couple, two

pal friend, companion, buddy, chum

palace castle, mansion, château

pale faint, colorless, wan, pallid bright

pamphlet booklet, brochure, leaflet, folder

pad (1)

palace

panic fear, fright, dread, alarm, terror

pants trousers, slacks

parade procession, march, display, review, pageant

parched dry, thirsty, arid, dehydrated

pardon forgive, excuse, absolve blame

part 1. portion, section, segment, piece

part 2. role, character

participate take part in, partake, contribute, join

particular fussy, critical, exacting

partner companion, associate, colleague, collaborator

party celebration, festivity

party

pass 1. do well, succeed fail

pass 2. deliver, hand over, transfer

pass 3. throw, toss, fling, hurl, pitch

passage corridor, lane, opening, channel

paste glue, mucilage, adhesive

patch mend, repair, fix

path route, way, track, trail, lane, road

patience tolerance, understanding, self-control
impatience

path

patriotic loyal, nationalistic

patrol watch, guard, protect, police

pattern 1. design, picture, print

pattern 2. model, example

78

pause   wait, stop, rest, recess   continue

peaceful   quiet, calm, still, serene   hectic

peak   top, crest, tip, summit   base

peculiar   odd, strange, unusual, queer   ordinary, normal

peddle   sell, vend, hawk

pedestrian   walker

peek   glance, look, glimpse

penalty   punishment, fine

penmanship   handwriting, script

pennant   flag, banner, streamer

pep   energy, spirit, vim, vigor

perfect   faultless, flawless, ideal, excellent   imperfect, defective

perform   do, carry out, achieve, accomplish

perhaps   maybe, possibly, conceivably

period   time, span, interval

perish   die, expire, succumb

permanent   steady, lasting, unchanging, constant   temporary

permit   allow, let, consent

personal   private, individual

perspire   sweat

persuade   win over, convince

peddle

pennant

pet (2)

pessimistic   unhappy, hopeless, gloomy, downhearted
optimistic

pester   annoy, bother, disturb, tease, nag, harass

pet   1. favorite, choice

pet   2. stroke, pat, caress, fondle

petite   little, small, slight, tiny   big

petrified   1. scared, frightened, terrified, horrified, shocked, stunned

petrified   2. hardened, stonelike, solidified

petty   unimportant, small, minor, trivial   important

phantom   ghost, spirit, vision, spook, fantasy, illusion

pharmacist   druggist, chemist

photograph   snapshot, picture

physician   doctor, medic

pick   choose, select, elect, opt

picture   illustration, drawing, representation

piece   part, portion, section, segment, bit, chunk, hunk

pier   dock, wharf

pierce   stab, puncture, penetrate

pile   heap, stack, mound, load, collection

pillow   cushion, headrest

pin   fasten, attach, clasp, clip

pioneer   settler, colonist

pistol   gun, revolver, firearm

picture

pitch   toss, fling, throw, hurl, cast

pity   sympathy, compassion

place   put, lay, set, deposit, arrange

plain   1. clear, simple, understandable, distinct
complicated

plain   2. unattractive, homely   pretty

plan   intend, aim, propose

playful   frisky, lively, gay, spirited, impish   serious

pleasant   pleasing, likable, appealing, agreeable,
cheerful, delightful, charming, satisfying
unpleasant

pledge   promise, vow, oath, agreement

plenty   a lot, sufficient, enough, ample   insufficient

plot   plan, scheme, concoct

plug   block, clog, stop, jam, obstruct   open, clear

plump   chubby, fat, stout, stocky, heavy, pudgy,
chunky   thin

plunge   dive, fall, plummet

poetry   rhyme, verse

point   direct, show, indicate

poisonous   toxic, deadly, venomous

poke   jab, push, shove, thrust

police   guard, watch, protect, defend, shield, secure,
patrol

polish

polish   shine, buff, rub, wax, glaze

polite   well-mannered, courteous, respectful, gracious
rude

poll   survey, vote, questionnaire

polluted   contaminated, impure, foul, dirty, poisoned
clean, pure

poor   penniless, needy, impoverished, destitute   rich

popular   1. common   unusual

popular   2. well-liked, favorite, admired   unpopular,
disliked

portable   movable, mobile, transferable   stationary

portion   part, section, segment, piece, share

position   1. place, spot, location

position   2. job, role, function

positive   sure, certain, definite   unsure

possessions   belongings, property

possible   likely, probable, feasible   impossible

post   1. list, notify, announce

post   2. job, position, duty, assignment

postpone   put off, delay, stall, procrastinate

pound   beat, strike, hit, punch, knock, rap, bang,
pummel

power   1. strength, might, force, vigor, energy

power   2. authority, control, influence

pound

82

practically   almost, nearly, approximately

practice   drill, exercise, train, rehearse

praise   compliment, commend, flatter

precious   1. valuable, expensive, costly, priceless
cheap

precious   2. special, loved, adored, cherished

precipitation   rain, snow, moisture

precise   exact, accurate, definite   approximate

predicament   mess, dilemma, plight

predict   forecast, foresee, prophesy

prefer   favor, like, fancy

prejudiced   partial, biased   fair, neutral

prepare   get ready, fix, arrange, concoct

present   gift, offering

present

preserve   keep, save, hold, maintain, conserve, protect,
guard   destroy, neglect

press   1. push, force, squeeze, clasp

press   2. iron, smooth

pretend   make believe, act, fake, bluff, feign

pretty   attractive, lovely, good-looking   homely,
unattractive

prevent   stop, block, keep from, deter   allow

price   cost, value, amount

pride   self-respect, self-esteem, dignity

primitive 1. original, ancient, prehistoric   modern

primitive 2. uncivilized, crude, barbaric

principal chief, main, leading

principle rule, law, belief

print publish, issue

prison jail, penitentiary, reformatory

private personal, secret, hidden, intimate   public

privilege advantage, right

prize award, reward, treasure

problem question, issue

procedure plan, practice, rule, policy, way, custom

proceed go ahead, progress, advance

produce make, create, manufacture

profession job, work, occupation, career, vocation

program schedule, plan, list, agenda

progress go ahead, proceed, advance

prohibit forbid, bar, ban, prevent   allow

project undertaking, enterprise, venture

promise agree, swear, pledge, guarantee, vow

promising hopeful, encouraging, favorable

prompt 1. punctual, on time   late

prompt 2. remind, coach, cue

proper correct, right, appropriate, fitting, decent, suitable   wrong, improper

property   possessions, holdings, belongings

prosperous   successful, comfortable, well-off, rich, wealthy, affluent   poor

protect   defend, safeguard, shield, support, cover

protest   object, complain, challenge

protest

proud   pleased, gratified

prove   show, demonstrate, document

provide   supply, give, furnish

provoke   annoy, bother, disturb, tease, taunt, irritate, anger, antagonize

pry   1. meddle, mix, snoop

pry   2. loosen, jimmy

publish   print, issue

pull   tug, tow, draw, drag, yank, haul   push

punch   beat, strike, hit, pound, knock, batter, wallop, slug, pummel

pull

punctual   prompt, on time   late

puncture   pierce, stab, penetrate

punish   discipline, correct, chastise

pupil   student

purchase   buy, acquire   sell

purify   cleanse, clarify, refine, filter   soil, pollute

purpose   goal, aim, object, target

push   press, thrust, shove, force, nudge   pull

pupil

put   place, lay, set, deposit
puzzle   mystery, problem, enigma

Q

quarrel

quaint   charming, old-fashioned
quake   shake, tremble, vibrate, shudder
qualified   able, capable, fit, competent, suited   unfit
quality   trait, feature, characteristic
quantity   amount, sum, number
quarrel   argue, fight, disagree, differ, dispute, bicker   agree
queer   odd, strange, peculiar, unusual, weird   normal
question   ask, inquire, interrogate   answer
quick   1. fast, rapid, swift, speedy   slow
quick   2. bright, alert, smart, sharp, keen   dull, slow
quiet   silent, still, hushed   noisy
quit   stop, end, cease, halt, conclude, discontinue, finish   continue
quiver   shake, tremble, shiver
quiz   test, examination
quote   repeat, echo, cite

86

R

race 1. run, speed, rush, dash, hurry, sprint

race 2. nationality, ancestry

racket 1. noise, commotion, uproar, hubbub, din, clamor, disturbance quiet

racket 2. fraud, swindle

rage 1. anger, violence, frenzy, furor, fit

rage 2. fad, style, fashion

ragged torn, worn, shabby, tattered, frayed, seedy

raid attack, invade, assault

raise 1. lift, elevate, boost, hoist lower

raise 2. produce, rear

rake collect, gather

rank grade, class, position

rapid fast, swift, speedy, quick, hasty slow

rare scarce, uncommon, unusual, unique common

rate grade, evaluate, rank, appraise

raw uncooked cooked

race (1)

ray light, beam, gleam

react respond, answer

ready prepared, set unprepared

real genuine, true, authentic, actual fake

realize understand, grasp, comprehend

rear 1. back, hind front

rear 2. raise, produce

reason explanation, cause, motive, basis, justification

reasonable fair, sensible, just, sound, practical, realistic, rational unreasonable, unfair

rebel disobey, defy, riot, revolt obey

recall remember, recollect, review, reminisce forget

receive take in, get, gain, obtain give

recent new, modern, current, up-to-date, late old

recess pause, stop, rest

recipe instructions, directions, formula

recite tell, relate, narrate, repeat

reckless careless, sloppy, thoughtless, rash, hasty, wild, inconsiderate careful

recognize know, acknowledge

recommend suggest, advise, advocate

record write, list, enter, log

recover 1. get back, regain, rescue, reclaim, retrieve lose

recover 2. get better, improve, heal, rally, recuperate

record

88

recreation   play, amusement, entertainment, pleasure, enjoyment, fun

reduce   decrease, lessen, cut   increase

referee   judge, umpire, mediator

reform   improve, change, revise

refrigerate   cool, chill

refund   repay, reimburse

regal   royal, majestic, stately, noble, grand

region   district, area, section, location, territory, vicinity, zone

referee

register   sign up, enlist, enroll, join

regular   common, ordinary, usual, familiar, everyday, typical, normal   unusual

rehearse   drill, train, practice, repeat, prepare

reject   discard, refuse, exclude, eliminate, bar   accept

relate   tell, recite, narrate, repeat, report, state, recount

related   connected, associated, akin

relax   rest, unwind

release   let go, dismiss, discharge, free   hold

reliable   dependable, trustworthy   unreliable

relief   1. help, assistance, aid

relief   2. ease, alleviation

relief   3. change, substitution, replacement, alternate

relax

religious pious, devout

rely depend, count

remain stay, continue

remark statement, comment

remarkable extraordinary, great, special, unusual, exceptional, noteworthy, memorable ordinary

remedy cure, treatment, relief

remember recall, recollect, review, reminisce forget

remove take away, eliminate, discard, withdraw leave

rent lease, let, hire

repair mend, fix, adjust, patch, restore, service break

repeat duplicate, echo

reply answer, response

report tell, recite, narrate, state, describe, recount

request ask for, apply for

require need, lack, want

rescue

rescue save, recover, free, salvage

research exploration, investigation, inquiry, probe

resemblance likeness, similarity

reserve keep, save, hold, put aside

resign give up, leave, quit

respect admire, appreciate, value, honor

respond   reply, answer, react

responsible   reliable, dependable, trustworthy
irresponsible

rest   1. pause, relax, unwind

rest   2. remains, balance, leftovers

restless   impatient, edgy, uneasy, fidgety   calm,
composed

restore   renew, renovate, repair

restriction   limitation, restraint

result   outcome, end, effect, consequence

retire   resign, leave, quit

return   1. go back, revisit

return   2. give back, repay

reunion   get-together, gathering, meeting

reveal   show, expose, display, disclose   hide

review   study, remember, recall, learn

revive   bring back, resuscitate

revolution   1. revolt, riot, rebellion, uprising

revolution   2. circle, orbit

reward   award, payment, prize, compensation

rhythm   beat, tempo

rich   wealthy, comfortable, well-to-do, affluent, prosperous   poor

rip

road

ridiculous   foolish, silly, stupid, outrageous, absurd, unbelievable   sensible

right   correct, accurate, good, fitting, suitable, proper, valid, sound   wrong

rigid   stiff, firm, unbending, hard   soft, flexible

rim   edge, border, frame, fringe

riot   rebellion, revolt, uprising, brawl

rip   tear, cut, split, slit, slash

ripe   ready, developed, mature, full-grown   green, undeveloped

risk   chance, gamble

road   path, route, way, thoroughfare

roam   wander, drift, meander, ramble, rove

rob   steal, loot, burglarize

role   part, character

room   space, leeway

rot   spoil, decay

rotate   spin, turn, gyrate, swivel, pivot

rough   1. bumpy, coarse, uneven, jagged, choppy   smooth

rough   2. crude, harsh, rowdy, tough   gentle

route   course, path, rounds

routine   habit, system, custom, practice, pattern

rove roam, wander, drift, meander, ramble

row 1. line, series, column, string

row 2. paddle

rowdy rough, disorderly, disobedient, boisterous well-behaved

royal regal, majestic, stately, noble, grand

rubbish waste, garbage, trash, refuse, scrap, junk

rubbish

rude impolite, disrespectful, discourteous, crude, ill-mannered, curt, insolent polite

rug carpet, mat

ruin spoil, destroy, wreck, demolish, ravage

rule 1. govern, control, regulate, command, manage, head, lead, supervise, direct, run, guide

rule 2. regulation, law

rumor gossip, talk

run 1. race, hurry, hasten, jog, sprint

run 2. govern, control, regulate, command, manage, head, lead, supervise, direct

run 3. operate, work

run 4. flow, stream, pour, gush

run 5. campaign, electioneer

rush hurry, hasten, speed, dash, hustle

rusty corroded

ruthless cruel, mean, heartless, brutal, savage kind

S

sacred religious, holy, spiritual

sad unhappy, depressed, downhearted, blue, sorrowful, downcast, gloomy, glum, forlorn, dejected, melancholy happy

safe secure, protected, guarded dangerous

sag droop, hang, drag

salary pay, wages, compensation

sample test, try, experiment

sand scrape, smooth, file, grind

sane sound, rational, sensible, logical

sanitary clean, hygienic, sterile dirty, unsanitary

sarcastic cutting, bitter, sharp, stinging

satisfied pleased, content, gratified displeased

save 1. keep, preserve, conserve, store, accumulate spend, discard

save 2. rescue, recover, retrieve

say speak, tell, declare, state, exclaim, express, remark, comment, mention, utter

scald burn, scorch

scar blemish, mark, wound

scarce rare, scanty, sparse plentiful

scare frighten, alarm, startle, shock, unnerve, terrify calm, soothe

scatter spread, disperse, distribute gather

scene view, sight, setting, picture, vista

scent odor, smell, aroma, fragrance

schedule program, plan, list, agenda, slate, line-up

scheme plot, plan, conspiracy

scold reprimand, chide, admonish

scold

scorch burn, singe, sear, char

score count, sum, tally, total

scoundrel rascal, devil, imp, scamp, villain

scout hunt, seek, search

scramble mix, blend, combine, jumble separate

scrap 1. small amount, shred, speck, fragment

scrap 2. litter, rubbish, junk, trash, garbage, waste, debris

scrape rub

scrape

scratch cut, mark, scrape, scar

scream yell, howl, cry, shout, screech, wail, shriek

screech shriek, scream, yell, howl, cry, shout, wail, squeal

95

seal (3)

screen guard, shield, net

scribble scrawl, scratch

script writing, penmanship

scrub scour, clean, rub, wash

sculpture carve, mold, shape, form, chisel

seal 1. fasten, secure, bind, close, shut open

seal 2. stamp, sign, mark

seal 3. sea lion

sear scorch, burn, singe, char

search scout, hunt, seek

season flavor, spice

secret private, hidden, secluded

section part, portion, segment, piece

secure safe, protected, guarded unsafe, insecure

seek search, scout, hunt

seem appear, look

seep ooze, leak, trickle

segment section, part, portion, piece, division

seize grab, grasp, snatch, clutch release

seldom rarely, hardly, infrequently often

select choose, pick, opt

self-conscious shy, timid, bashful, embarrassed
confident

selfish self-centered, greedy, possessive generous,
good-natured

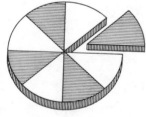

segment

96

sell peddle, vend buy

send dispatch, forward, transmit receive

sensational marvelous, wonderful, extraordinary, glorious, great, grand, magnificent, splendid, superb, divine, spectacular, exciting, thrilling ordinary, dull

senseless foolish, silly, dumb, stupid, inane sensible

sensible reasonable, logical, practical, realistic, wise, intelligent foolish

separate divide, split, part, sort, isolate join, unite

sequel follow-up, continuation

serious 1. solemn, grave, somber, grim gay, carefree

serious 2. important, major, significant, meaningful unimportant

sermon lecture, talk

serpent snake, viper

serpent

set 1. place, put, lay, deposit, arrange

set 2. fix, adjust, regulate

settle 1. decide, resolve, reconcile

settle 2. locate, occupy, live

several many, numerous, various, some few

severe harsh, cruel, hard, rough, tough, extreme mild

shabby ragged, torn, worn, shoddy, tattered, frayed, seedy

shack

shack   hut, cabin, shanty

shake   tremble, shudder, shiver, quiver, vibrate

shameful   awful, disgraceful, humiliating, scandalous

shampoo   soap, lather, wash

shape   form, make, develop, fashion, create, construct, mold, design

share   divide, split, distribute, apportion

sharp   1. pointy, angular dull

sharp   2. bright, clever, smart, alert, quick-witted, keen, shrewd dull, slow

shatter   break, fracture, crack, crush, split, smash, destroy

shelter   1. housing, quarters

shelter   2. protection, cover, refuge

shield   protect, defend, safeguard, cover, screen expose

shine   glow, gleam, beam, sparkle, glimmer, glisten

shiver   shake, tremble, shudder, quiver

shock   startle, surprise, stun, jar

shoot   fire

shop   buy, purchase

shore   coast, beach, waterfront

short   1. little, small, puny tall

short   2. brief, concise, succinct long

shampoo

shore

98

shortage lack, want, need, absence, deficiency
abundance

shout scream, yell, howl, cry, call

shove push, bump, nudge

show 1. demonstrate, illustrate, indicate, explain,
clarify

show 2. performance, presentation, production,
exhibit

shrewd sharp, bright, clever, smart, alert, crafty,
quick-witted, keen, sly dull, slow

shriek scream, yell, howl, cry, shout, screech, wail

shrink become smaller, shrivel, wither grow, expand

shudder tremble, shake, shiver, quiver

shuffle mix, scramble, jumble

shut close, fasten, lock, seal open

shy bashful, timid, modest, coy aggressive

sick ill, ailing well, healthy

sight view, scene, vista, picture, spectacle

sign 1. endorse, write, mark

sign 2. signal, motion, gesture, indication

silent quiet, still, hushed noisy

silly foolish, senseless, inane sensible

simple 1. easy, clear, uncomplicated difficult

simple 2. plain, ordinary

sin   evil, crime, offense

sincere   honest, truthful, genuine, unaffected   phony

sing   vocalize, chant

singe   sear, burn, scorch, char

site   place, location, area, spot, region

situation   case, condition, circumstance

skillful   handy, expert, clever, capable, apt, adept   awkward

skinny

skimpy   sparse, scanty, scarce   generous

skinny   thin, lean, scrawny, slim   chubby

skip   pass over, leave out, omit, miss, exclude   include

slam   close, bang, shut

slant   slope, tilt, incline

slap   hit, smack, strike

slash   slit, cut, sever, gash

slavery   captivity, bondage   freedom

slay   kill, murder, slaughter, exterminate, destroy

sleep   doze, nap, snooze, slumber

slice   cut, carve, slit

slide   glide, skid, slip

sling   splint, support, bandage

slide

slip   1. slide, skid

slip   2. error, mistake, oversight, blunder

slit   slash, cut, split, gash

slope   slant, incline, tilt

sloppy   careless, messy, untidy, slovenly   neat

slow   1. sluggish, delaying   fast

slow   2. dull, stupid, dim-witted   bright

sly   shrewd, sneaky, crafty, underhanded, shifty

smack   slap, hit, strike, crack, whack, wallop

small   little, slight, puny   big

smart   1. intelligent, bright, alert, wise, clever, quick   stupid

smart   2. pain, ache, hurt

smash   shatter, break, crack, split, destroy, demolish

smash

smear   1. smudge, soil, spot, stain

smear   2. spread, coat, dab

smell   scent, odor, aroma, fragrance

smile   grin, smirk   frown

smog   fog, haziness, cloudiness

smooth   polished, sleek, even   rough

smother   suffocate, muffle, stifle, choke

smudge   smear, soil, spot, stain

snake   serpent, viper

snatch   grab, seize, grasp, clutch   release

snug   cozy, comfortable, secure

soil (2)

soak wet, drench, saturate dry

soap lather, shampoo

sob cry, weep, bawl

sociable friendly, cordial unfriendly

soft delicate, tender, fluffy, flexible hard

soggy damp, wet, moist, watery dry

soil 1. dirty, spot, stain, smudge, smear

soil 2. ground, earth, dirt

solemn sad, serious, grave, somber, grim, gloomy, glum happy

solid hard, firm, rigid, inflexible, sturdy, strong soft, flimsy

solution answer, explanation, finding, outcome, result

solve answer, explain, figure out

song tune, melody

soon shortly, promptly, presently

soothe calm, comfort, pacify

sore painful, aching, tender

sorrow sadness, grief, trouble, misfortune, suffering, misery joy

sorry apologetic, remorseful

sort arrange, organize, classify, group, categorize

sound noise

souvenir remembrance, keepsake, memento, token

spacious roomy, broad, vast narrow

spar box, fight

sparkle shine, flash, glimmer, glitter, glisten, twinkle

speak talk, comment

special unusual, exceptional, notable, outstanding, extraordinary, remarkable ordinary

spectacular dramatic, sensational, marvelous, wonderful, extraordinary, glorious, great, grand, magnificent, splendid, superb, exciting, thrilling ordinary, dull

speedy fast, rapid, swift, quick, hasty

spend pay out, use save

spice season, flavor

spin turn, twirl, rotate, pivot

spirit courage, nerve, spunk

spiteful mean, malicious, vindictive

splendid glorious, great, grand, magnificent, superb, majestic, wonderful, divine, sensational, marvelous, fine, excellent

split crack, break, separate, divide

spoil 1. damage, harm, hurt, destroy, ruin, upset, impair

spoil 2. rot, decay

sponsor backer, supporter, promoter

spin

103

spot (1)

stage

spook   ghost, spirit, phantom

spot   1. soil, dirty, stain, smudge, smear

spot   2. pick out, recognize, identify, spy, sight, distinguish

spread   1. unfold, stretch out, sprawl

spread   2. distribute, scatter, disperse

spry   lively, active, energetic, spirited, agile, nimble   sluggish

squad   group, gang, crew

squander   waste, throw away   save

squash   crush, squeeze, mash

squeeze   press, pinch, crush

squirt   spurt, splash, spray, spout

stab   pierce, puncture, penetrate, perforate

stack   pile, heap, mound, load

stage   platform, podium

stain   dirty, spot, soil, smudge, smear, discolor

stale   old, spoiled   fresh

stall   delay, postpone, procrastinate

stammer   stutter, falter

stamp   1. seal, mark, label

stamp   2. pound, bang

stampede   rush, panic

stand   1. rise, get up

stand 2. stay, remain, continue

stand 3. suffer, bear, tolerate

stand 4. base, pedestal

stand 5. booth, kiosk

stanza verse, measure

staple attach, fasten, join, connect

star 1. lead, headliner

star 2. heavenly body

stare look, gaze, gape, gawk, glare

start begin, commence, launch   end

startle shock, surprise, stun, frighten, upset

starvation hunger, famine

state declare, say, exclaim, announce, tell, express, relate, report

statement account, report, announcement, declaration

station

station stop, depot

stationary fixed, firm, immovable   movable

stationery paper, writing materials

statue figure, sculpture

stay remain, continue, stand

steady regular, constant, continuous   changing

steal rob, take, burglarize

steam vapor, gas, smoke

statue

105

steer   drive, handle, direct, manage, conduct, lead, head, command, run

step   walk, tread

sterilize   clean, sanitize, disinfect

stern   strict, harsh, rough, tough, hard, severe, firm   lenient, easygoing

stick   attach, adhere, cling

stiff   rigid, firm, unbending, hard, inflexible   flexible

still   quiet, calm, peaceful, serene, tranquil   noisy

sting   prick, wound

stingy   cheap, tight, miserly   generous

stink   smell, odor, stench

stir   mix, blend, combine, scramble

stock   supply, collection, reserve, inventory

stomach   belly, abdomen

stone   rock, pebble

stool

stool   seat, chair

stop   cease, end, halt, quit, conclude, discontinue   start

store   1. keep, stock, collect, save

store   2. shop, market

storm   gale, hurricane, tornado

story   tale, account, narrative

stout   fat, chubby, plump, stocky   thin

106

strange   odd, unusual, peculiar, queer, weird, bizarre
  ordinary

strangle   choke, suffocate, smother

stray   wander, drift, roam, rove, meander

stream   creek, brook

street   road, avenue, thoroughfare

strength   power, force, might, energy, vigor
  weakness

stream

stretch   extend, spread, expand

strict   stern, harsh, tough, exact, severe, firm   lenient

strike   hit, bat, slap, smack, slug, swat, knock

strip   remove, uncover, peel, bare   cover

stripe   line, mark, streak

stroke   rub, pet, pat, caress, fondle

strong   mighty, powerful, sturdy, hardy, tough,
  healthy, rugged, robust, muscular   weak

struggle   battle, fight, feud, conflict

stubborn   obstinate, willful, headstrong, pigheaded,
  ornery   flexible

student   pupil

stuff   fill, load, pack, cram   empty

stumble   trip, tumble, flounder, falter

stun   shock, startle, surprise, daze

stunt   feat, act, performance, exploit

107

stupid   dumb, dull, silly, foolish, dim-witted   smart

stutter   stammer, falter

stylish   fashionable, well-dressed   drab

subject   topic, issue, theme, question, point, plot

substitute   replace, change, exchange, trade, switch

subtract   deduct, remove, withdraw   add

successful   prosperous, well-off, fortunate, winning
unsuccessful

sudden   unexpected, abrupt, hasty

sufficient   enough, plenty, adequate   insufficient

suffocate   smother, stifle, choke

suggestion   proposal, plan, offer

suitable   proper, fitting, correct, appropriate
improper

sum   total, quantity

summary   review, outline, accounting

sundown   sunset, dusk, evening, nightfall   sunrise

sunny   bright, cheerful, pleasant   dull

sunrise   dawn, daybreak, morning   sunset

sunset   sundown, dusk, evening, nightfall   sunrise

superb   excellent, fine, splendid, glorious, great, grand, magnificent, wonderful, divine, sensational, marvelous

supernatural   ghostly, mystical

supervise manage, direct, lead, guide, run, control, govern, command, head, boss

supply provide, give, furnish

support help, aid, assist, serve, encourage

suppose believe, think, imagine, consider

sure certain, positive, definite uncertain

surplus extra, additional, spare, leftover, excess shortage

surprise astonish, astound, amaze, startle, shock, stun

surrender give up, quit, yield

surround encircle, wrap

survive live, remain, last

suspect doubt, question, mistrust, distrust trust

suspense uncertainty, uneasiness, anxiety

suspension 1. removal, dismissal

suspension 2. interruption, break, pause, intermission

swap trade, exchange, switch, barter

swat hit, strike, smack, whack

sway swing, rock, reel, swagger

swear 1. promise, vow, pledge, guarantee

swear 2. curse

sweep clean, brush, vacuum

sweet 1. charming, lovely, pleasant, agreeable, adorable disagreeable

swing

sword

sweet   2. sugary

swift   speedy, fast, rapid, quick, hasty   slow

swindle   cheat, trick, defraud, bamboozle

swing   sway, rock, hang, dangle

switch   change, exchange, swap, trade, substitute

sword   knife, blade

symbol   token, emblem

sympathy   understanding, pity, compassion

symptom   sign, mark, indication

system   method, plan, manner, means, way, style, procedure

T

tactful   thoughtful, considerate, kind, sensitive, diplomatic   tactless

tag   1. follow, shadow, trail, pursue, tail

tag   2. label, name, brand

tail   1. follow, shadow, trail, pursue, tag

tail   2. back, rear, end

110

take 1. seize, capture, get, obtain give

take 2. carry, bring, transport

tale story, account

talent ability, skill, know-how, gift, forte

talk speak, discuss, converse

tall 1. big, large short

tall 2. high, lofty small

tame gentle, obedient, mild, domesticated wild

tangle twist, knot, snarl

tantrum fit, outburst, flare-up

tap 1. rap, pat

tap 2. faucet, spigot

tap (2)

tape 1. wrap, bind, tie

tape 2. record

target aim, goal, object, purpose

tart sour, sharp, bitter, pungent sweet

task chore, job, work, assignment, duty

taste sample, test, try, savor

tavern inn, bar, saloon, pub

tax duty, toll, tariff

taxi cab, hack

taxi

teach instruct, show, educate, inform, tell, advise, tutor

team gang, group, crew, band

tear rip, cut, split, slit, slash

tease annoy, bother, pester, badger, provoke

televise telecast, broadcast

tell relate, recite, narrate, report, state, explain, in-form, convey

temperamental moody, sensitive, touchy

temporary passing, momentary, short-lived, transient
permanent

tenant occupant, resident

tense nervous, anxious, strained, uptight, rigid
relaxed

term period, time, duration

terrible horrible, horrid, dreadful, awful, atrocious
wonderful

terrific marvelous, wonderful, glorious, great, mag-nificent, splendid, superb, sensational ordinary

terrify frighten, scare, alarm, horrify, shock, petrify

territory region, district, area, section, zone

test 1. examine, question, quiz

test 2. try, sample, experiment, attempt

thankful grateful, appreciative

thaw melt, defrost

theater playhouse, hall

theater

thick   broad, bulky, solid   thin

thief   robber, burglar, crook

thin   skinny, lean, slim, slender   fat

think   1. believe, suppose, imagine, expect, guess, suspect, assume

think   2. consider, reflect, ponder

thirsty   dry, parched, dehydrated

thorough   complete, all-out, intensive   incomplete

thought   1. idea, notion, concept

thought   2. care, attention, regard, concern

thoughtful   considerate, kind, sympathetic   thoughtless

thoughtless   inconsiderate, unkind   thoughtful

threaten   warn, bully, intimidate, bulldoze, terrorize, harass

thrifty   economical, careful, frugal   wasteful

thrilling   exciting, delightful, enchanting, stirring, moving, breathtaking   boring

throw   pitch, toss, fling, hurl, cast

throw

ticket   1. pass, voucher

ticket   2. summons, subpoena, citation

tidy   neat, orderly, well-kept, trim   sloppy

tie   fasten, secure, bind, wrap   untie

tight   snug, firm   loose

tilt   slope, slant, incline

timid   shy, bashful, reserved, meek   bold

tint   color, dye, stain

tiny   little, small, minute, puny   huge

tip   1. end, point, extremity

tip   2. gratuity, bonus

tip   3. advice, information, clue

tired   exhausted, weary, fatigued   rested

title   name, heading

toll   charge, fee, fare

tone   sound, pitch, key

tool   instrument, device, implement, utensil, gadget

top   head, peak, tip, summit   bottom

topic   subject, issue, theme, question, point

topple   fall, drop, tumble, collapse

torch   light, lantern

tornado   windstorm, tempest

torture   agony, pain, torment

toss   throw, pitch, fling, hurl, cast

total   1. whole, entire, complete   partial

total   2. add, sum up, count

touch   feel, handle, contact

tough   1. hardy, strong, sturdy, rugged, robust   weak

torch

tornado

tough   2. hard, difficult, rough, complicated   easy

tour   trip, excursion, journey

tournament   contest, game, match, competition

tow   pull, haul, drag, tug

toxic   poisonous, deadly, venomous

trace   copy, reproduce, duplicate, outline

track   path, trail, road, course

trade   1. exchange, barter, switch, swap, bargain

trade   2. business, work, line, employment

tradition   custom, habit

tragic   sad, disastrous, unfortunate, dreadful

trail   1. follow, chase, tail, track, pursue

trail   2. track, path, road, course

train   1. teach, drill, practice, exercise, prepare, condition, groom

train   2. railroad cars

train (2)

traitor   betrayer, spy, informer

tramp   vagrant, hobo, vagabond

transfer   hand over, deliver, pass, change

translate   interpret

trap   catch, capture, seize, hook, snare   release

trash   rubbish, waste, garbage, refuse, scrap, junk, litter, debris

travel   journey, tour

treasure   1. adore, idolize, cherish, appreciate, value

treasure   2. fortune, wealth, riches

treat   1. deal with, handle, regard, tend to

treat   2. delight, pleasure, thrill

treaty   pact, agreement, understanding, alliance

tremble   shake, shudder, quiver

tremendous   gigantic, colossal, huge, giant, vast, enormous, immense   tiny

trial   1. test, experiment, tryout

trial   2. court case

tribe   group, clan, sect

trick   deceive, mislead, fool, dupe

trim   1. cut, shave, pare

trim   2. decorate, beautify, adorn

trip   1. stumble, tumble, fall, falter

trip   2. tour, journey, excursion

troop   group, company, squad, unit

trophy

trophy   award, prize, reward

trouble   bother, difficulty, inconvenience

truant   absentee

truce   armistice

true   genuine, real, pure, authentic, actual, valid, right, proper, correct, accurate, exact   false

trust   believe, accept   distrust

try   test, sample, experiment, attempt
tug   pull, tow, drag, yank, haul
tumble   fall, topple, drop
tune   melody, song
tunnel   passage, channel
turn   rotate, spin, swivel, pivot, twist
tutor   teach, instruct, coach
twinkle   sparkle, shine, glimmer, glitter, glisten, gleam

tumble

twirl   turn, spin, twist, whirl
twist   turn, twirl, spin
twitch   jerk, shudder, spasm
type   kind, sort, variety, class, category, group, species
tyrant   dictator, taskmaster, slave driver

U

umpire

ugly   homely, unattractive, hideous   beautiful
umpire   referee, judge, mediator
unable   unfit, incapable, powerless   able
unanimous   agreed, in accord, harmonious
unaware   ignorant, unknowing   aware

117

unbelievable 1. incredible, absurd, fantastic

unbelievable 2. doubtful, questionable, suspicious
believable

uncertain doubtful, unsure, undecided, unpredictable
certain

unchanged same, steady, constant changed

uncivilized savage, wild, unrefined civilized

uncomfortable awkward, cramped, unpleasant
comfortable

uncommon unusual, rare, scarce, unique, different,
novel, original common

unconscious out cold, senseless, comatose
conscious

unconstitutional unlawful, illegal legal

uncover reveal, show, expose, disclose cover,
conceal

undecided uncertain, doubtful, unsure, indefinite,
vague certain

under below, beneath above, over

understand follow, see, know, appreciate, grasp,
comprehend

undress unclothe, disrobe, strip dress

unemployed jobless, idle, unoccupied employed

unexpected sudden, unforeseen, unplanned
expected

unfair unjust, partial fair

unfaithful untrue, disloyal, fickle faithful

unfamiliar strange, unusual, new, different
familiar

unfortunate unlucky, sad, unhappy fortunate

unfriendly antisocial, cool, distant, aloof friendly

ungrateful unappreciative, thankless grateful

unhappy sad, depressed, dejected, downhearted, blue,
sorrowful, downcast, gloomy, glum, forlorn, melancholy happy

unhappy

unhealthy sickly, ill, ailing, frail, weak healthy

uniform outfit, costume

unimportant petty, minor, trivial, insignificant
important

unnecessary needless, useless, uncalled-for
necessary

unoccupied vacant, available, open, empty occupied

unpack unload, empty pack

unpleasant nasty, disagreeable, unlikable, offensive,
obnoxious pleasant

unpopular disliked, unwanted popular

unreasonable ridiculous, absurd, extreme
reasonable

unruly disorderly, wild, disobedient orderly

119

unsafe   dangerous, risky, hazardous   safe

unsatisfactory   poor, inferior, second-rate, inadequate   satisfactory

unsuccessful   failing, unfortunate   successful

untie   loosen, undo, unfasten   tie

unusual   uncommon, rare, unique, different, novel, original   usual

unwilling   opposed, reluctant   willing

uphold   support, maintain, defend, back

upright   1. standing, erect, vertical

upright   2. honorable, respectable, moral

uprising   revolution, revolt, riot, rebellion

uproar   noise, racket, clamor, commotion, disturbance, tumult, hubbub   peace

upset   disturb, annoy, bother, unnerve   soothe

urge   push, press, advise, prod, coax, prompt   discourage

urgent   necessary, important, essential, vital, crucial   unimportant

useful   helpful, practical, handy, valuable, beneficial   useless

useless   worthless   useful

usher

usher   guide, escort

usual   common, regular, normal, ordinary, familiar, everyday, typical   unusual

V

vacant   unoccupied, available, open, empty   filled, occupied

vacation   leave, break, recess, holiday

valuable   important, significant, precious, costly, expensive

value   worth, cost

vandalism   destruction, ruination

vanish   disappear, fade   appear

vapor   steam, fog, mist

various   several, different, many, numerous, assorted

vary   change, alter

vast   huge, immense, enormous, great   tiny

vegetation   plants, growth, flora

vegetation

verdict   decision, ruling, finding, judgment

verse   1. poetry, rhyme

verse   2. passage, section, part, division

version   account, story, description, interpretation

veto   refuse, deny   approve

121

vibrate   shake, quiver

vicious   ferocious, fierce, savage, brutal, cruel, ruthless, evil, wicked, mean

victim   loser, underdog, sufferer, prey

victory   triumph, success, winning   defeat

view   sight, scene, vista, picture

villain   scoundrel, rascal, devil

violate   break, disobey

violence   rage, anger, frenzy, fury

vision   1. eyesight, perception

vision   2. image, illusion, fantasy, dream

volunteer   offer, come forward

vote   ballot, choice, selection

voyage   journey, cruise, crossing

W

wake

wag   wave, flap, swing, shake

wake   get up, arise

walk   stroll

wallop   smack, slap, hit, strike, crack, whack, thrash, beat, slug

wander   stray, drift, roam, rove, ramble

want   desire, wish for, long for, crave

war   battle, fight, feud, struggle, combat, conflict

warn   1. caution, inform, notify, alert

warn   2. threaten

wash   launder, clean, scrub

waste   squander, misuse   save

watch   1. observe, see, look at

watch   2. guard, protect, defend, shield

wave   sway, move, flap

wax   polish, shine, glaze

weak   feeble, frail, powerless   strong

wealthy   rich, comfortable, well-to-do, affluent, prosperous   poor

wed   marry, join, unite

weird   queer, odd, strange, peculiar, unusual, creepy, spooky, eerie   normal

welcome   greet, receive

whack   wallop, smack, slap, hit, strike, crack, thrash, beat, slug

whip   strike, beat, thrash, flog, crack

whole   complete, total, entire   partial

wicked   evil, bad, sinful, mean, cruel, ruthless, vicious   good, saintly

wide   broad, expansive   narrow

wash

wed

win

wife spouse, mate, married woman

wig hairpiece

wild 1. untamed, uncivilized, savage, ferocious
civilized, tame

wild 2. reckless, rash, crazy, frenzied calm

willing agreeable, ready, consenting unwilling

win succeed, triumph, prevail lose

1. wind air, breeze, gust

2. wind turn, twist, coil

wire telegraph, cable

wise smart, intelligent, clever, knowledgeable,
learned, educated, scholarly uneducated

wish desire, long for, want, crave

withdraw remove, subtract, deduct deposit

without lacking, wanting, needing, missing, minus,
less with

witty clever, amusing, funny, humorous

wonderful marvelous, glorious, great, grand, magnificent, splendid, superb, divine, sensational, spectacular horrible

woods forest

work 1. labor, toil

work 2. operate, run, manage, handle

workout exercise, practice, drill

124

world   universe, earth

worn   used, old, secondhand, ragged   new

worried   troubled, concerned, disturbed, upset, nervous   calm

worship   adore, idolize, cherish, revere

wound   injury, hurt, bruise

wrap   cover, bind, tie   uncover

wreath   garland

wreck   destroy, ruin, demolish

wring   squeeze, twist

wrong   incorrect, inaccurate, faulty, mistaken   right

wreath

X

x-ray   picture, photograph

Y

yacht   boat

yacht

125

yarn

yank pull, tug, jerk
yarn wool, thread
yell shout, scream, howl, cry, call, shriek, screech
yield 1. produce, give, provide, supply
yield 2. surrender, give up, sacrifice
young youthful, juvenile old
youngster child, minor, youth, kid

Z

zero nothing, nil, none
zone region, district, area, section, territory
zoo menagerie
zoom speed, zip, whiz, fly